Maladies of the Soul

Maladies
of the Soul

ISA KAMARI

Marshall Cavendish
Editions

Published in 2022 by Marshall Cavendish Editions
An imprint of Marshall Cavendish International

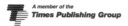
A member of the
Times Publishing Group

Other Marshall Cavendish Offices:
Marshall Cavendish Corporation, 800 Westchester Ave, Suite N-641,
Rye Brook, NY 10573, USA • Marshall Cavendish International (Thailand)
Co Ltd, 253 Asoke, 16th Floor, Sukhumvit 21 Road, Klongtoey Nua,
Wattana, Bangkok 10110, Thailand • Marshall Cavendish (Malaysia) Sdn
Bhd, Times Subang, Lot 46, Subang Hi-Tech Industrial Park, Batu Tiga,
40000 Shah Alam, Selangor Darul Ehsan, Malaysia

National Library Board, Singapore Cataloguing-in-Publication Data

Name(s): Isa Kamari, 1960-
Title: Maladies of the soul / Isa Kamari.
Description: Singapore : Marshall Cavendish Editions, 2022.
Identifier(s): ISBN 978-981-5044-35-5 (paperback)
Subject(s): LCSH: Social isolation--Fiction. | Alienation (Social
psychology)--Fiction.
Classification: DDC S823--dc23

Printed in Singapore

Contents

1

The Orchid

The path to the monastery is sheltered by rows of yellow sandalwood trees. The morning sunlight slips between the leaves and dances in the gentle breeze. Looking up, I see a wild orchid swaying from one of the branches. I stop for a moment. Its roots are wrapped around the branch. I am delighted by the soft white petals. The thick foliage offers a strong support for life. I look around me. There are no other orchids.

The fragrant damp air is soft and fresh. My chest swells and my heavy heart seems to lighten a little. I have decided to visit this particular monastery because of its location in the jungle. The wild orchid confirms my expectation that I would not be disappointed. I am leaving town for a while and do not want to be disturbed. My mind craves for balance and peace. It wants that calm without His presence. He is a ghost, and I had expunged Him from my dreams. The bruises on my forehead from bowing low in prayer are the only reminders of Him that are left to me. I hope that these bruises will just naturally fade away. Now I want to use nature as a way of finding myself. I am tired of those stupid stories from over 1,400 years ago.

Nevertheless, I still believe that the spiritual world is an integral part of life. The feeling of unease I have been experiencing these past few months have convinced me of that. But I don't want to connect those feelings with Him. I want to be at peace without Him. So, I am determined to seek spiritual consolation in this particular place. The monastery does not revere any of His particular names. It does not promote any particular teachings about Him. It simply offers a spiritual path that is unconnected to any of His manifestations or any teachings about His being. The monastery is a path to nothingness.

Closing my eyes, I begin to breathe deeply. The scent of the orchid surrounds me, and I delightedly take it into myself. The desires nestling in my mind seems to dissolve in that wonderful fragrance which even absorbs the perfume of the name of God. The emptiness that follows calms my heart and mind. I feel strange and isolated. My body briefly trembles. This is the first and last time. I will win. I will root Him out of my life.

I look up again so that I can secretly whisper something to the wild flower. The orchid is the only friend I have made these last few hours. I have no idea of how far I might have to travel or where. All I know is that I want to be free of my inner sickness. I want to be the way I used to be. Fresh and free, one with the world.

Even though the orchid is not as beautiful or as distinct as the hybrid orchids I have seen in the conservatory of the Botanic Gardens in my own country, it shines with an innocent radiance in these primal conditions. This wild orchid has never been disturbed by human desires or touched by rough hands. I do not know if my talking to it would destroy its peace and tranquillity.

I continue walking. According to my map, there is a waterfall on the other side of this hill. The air is becoming increasingly damp and cool, giving me greater confidence in the direction I am walking. I focus on the sounds around me. There is the gentle sound of water splashing in the distance.

I quicken my pace. The monastery is located on the side of a hill to the left of the waterfall. My heart beats faster and fills with hope and longing. I breathe deeply, trying to calm the storm that rages within me. From the little I had read of the teachings of this monastery, I should learn to control any manifestation of desire in my life. True happiness can only be achieved when a person is completely free of all cravings. That philosophy has drawn me here. Apparently, my first lesson has already begun.

Of course, there are many monasteries in this neighbouring country that promote these teachings. But this one is unique. It is under the authority of a local monk who has an excellent command of English. And it is the only monastery that would accept someone like me. In fact, it is extremely famous for its ability to cure those suffering from my particular sickness.

I admit that I am sick because I am unhappy. I am sure that physical, mental and spiritual health are the source of true happiness. And, to reach that state, I do not believe that I need any of God's official religions to cure me. In fact, I consider them to be the drug that has bewitched me and destroyed my mind and my soul all these years.

There are not many ways to healing that are open to me. I had filled in the application form and been absolutely honest in answering the various questions asked by the programme administrator. I feel lucky to have been accepted.

I look to the right. A tree had recently fallen to the ground. The large fragments of its bark are still red. I have a sense that part of the trunk had been burned. The smell of smoke hangs in the air. The leaves on the smaller surrounding trees are still green. Perhaps the fallen tree had been struck by lightning.

I am startled. My body trembles. I look up to see whether there might be a return of the rain and lightning. I know that one has to be careful walking through the jungle in this particular region. But the soft rays of the sun warm my brow and drive away my fears. I feel reassured.

A moment later, I experience a feeling of horror. My breathing stops for a moment. Would I suffer the same fate as that tree? Would my actions bring about His anger and punishment? I think about this for a moment and then smile cynically. If I don't believe in Him, why should I fear His wrath? The process of recovery has to begin with the sincere desire to remove Him from my heart and mind. As long as He remains in my thoughts and feelings, I would never be cured.

I am absolutely determined to conquer my inner gloom by using the most suitable means available. Even when nature is attacked, it always revives and grows more vigorous again. I want to be like that. I believe that nature will always win in the end. And I am a part of nature.

The sound of the waterfall is closer now. My spirit quickly revives. No one can interfere with my determination to find new happiness. I have almost reached my destination.

The monastery is perched on the side of the hill. Its simple architecture reminds me of the need to be humble in my own eyes. Especially as I am only a visitor here. I need to learn to accept the situation as it is, most particularly the knowledge of my own weakness.

A yellow butterfly approaches me and lands on my arm. I am glad that my presence in this place has been accepted. The butterfly then opens its wings again and flies away. I continue on my way. Without my knowing it, the butterfly has been leading me along the track through the jungle. It is a clear sign that I would be guided in my search.

Looking up, I see a monk standing at the end of the track. He is smiling gently. His face shines like the yellow glow of his robes. His calm eyes immediately reassure me. Unconsciously, I wave at him, then, shortly afterwards, smile back at him.

"Welcome, Helmy," he says in English as he raises his two hands together to his chest in a respectful greeting.

"Thank you, your holiness."

"Just call me by my name, Bunag," he replies gently, adjusting his robes.

"Fine, Bunag."

His lips form a smile. His eyes shine innocently. A moment later, I hear the rustle of leaves on the ground. Bunag looks past me. He seems slightly surprised. I turn around and see another monk approaching us. He is walking with his head bowed. From the colour of his bald head and the brightness of the skin on his arms, I guess that he does not come from around this district. His head remains bowed as he approaches us. I look at Bunag. He smiles broadly and gently pats me on the shoulder.

"Allow me to introduce Antonio," he says.

For some reason, my heart begins to beat more quickly when I hear his name. The second monk raises his head and looks at me. Smiling, he lifts his hands and politely greets me.

I am startled by the calm expression on his face. His clear blue eyes fascinate me. Cold sweat covers my forehead. My body trembles. To be honest, I have never seen a man as handsome as Antonio.

"Antonio, this is Helmy," Bunag continues. "He comes from Singapore."

"Welcome," Antonio says in a soft deep voice.

Unable to speak, I stare at his face. My heart beats more quickly. The hairs on my arms stand up. My stomach tightens. I feel sexually aroused.

It is clear that I would face my greatest temptation right here. I have left my hometown to escape my continual involvement with such base instincts. Without my realising it, they have followed me here.

I am struck by doubt. I am no longer sure that I can be cured of my long sickness. "God, is this how You have decided to curse me?"

To my surprise, the butterfly reappears and settles once more on my sleeve. I am briefly startled. Suddenly, I feel like a strange hybrid orchid growing in God's wild jungle.

2

The Bargaining

"Allahuakbar!"

To whom should I focus my attention in this prostration?

"God Most Pure, Most High and Most Glorious."

Is that the voice of the Imam in front of me or the murmur of my heart? Surely it is not the whisper of Satan. Can I be sure?

"Assalamualaikum warahmatullah."

Relieved. Not because of the serenity that resides in those spoken words, but because the words are uttered at last.

To whom are the supplications by the Imam directed? To the living or the dead? For what purpose? To bless the life in this world or secure salvation in the hereafter? What separates here and hereafter? Time? What connects them both? Time again? Time which is of yesterday, today and tomorrow? Or time as Pure Duration?

My body posits itself in the mosque but my mind is wandering aimlessly. Some have suggested that time stands still in the bowing and prostrating, but it is obvious that the beads of moments have been let loose and scattered in my mind. I do not feel the eternity or peace of an obedient and devoted servant. If I were to die at this moment, would I still be able to enjoy bliss in heaven? Am I not in a sacred place after all?

Is it fair to determine one's fate based on the deed at the last breath? Would it be a good or bad ending? If so, what is the value of an entire life before the fateful moment? What is the meaning of loyal faith and sustained devotion? What is the use of good deeds if they are to be annulled by a moment of indiscretion at the end?

This mosque is but a symbol, empty although full of congregants. So, why am I here? There is a strange force that brings me here by coercion, or perhaps persuasion. I am not sure whether it is pushing me forward or pulling me backwards. Or am I at the mercy of its whim and fancy? Whose are those? Is this Fate?

"Where to?" A voice interrupts my ponderings.

I turn my head and see the Imam approaching me.

"Nowhere in particular, Sir."

He smiles. "No worries. Allah will guide you. Just ask Him."

I smile nonchalantly and shake his hand. Suddenly, I feel a deep sense of sorrow from my parting salutations that were meant to be polite for their own sake.

The handphone in my pocket vibrates. I had forgotten to switch it off during prayer. It is fortunate that it did not disturb the congregants, as it would have if someone had called or sent a message to me then. I smile cynically. Actually, it was me who had switched off during the prayer. Now I am awakened by the notification of an inanimate object.

I read the WhatsApp message: "150/90/2". It is the answer to my query sent before I had stepped into the mosque. I take out my wallet and check its contents. There is only $120.

What shall I do? Head to that place? I look at my watch: 4.45pm. It is still early. Maybe I'll go later, if I still have the desire.

I walk to Bussorah Street. My eyes scan to the right and left.

"Come over, boss, try some Turkish food. It's delicious, like those in heaven."

I pause. I'm not hungry or in the mood to try any heavenly food.

Then I see Wardah bookshop. I walk towards and enter the shop without giving the customary Islamic salutation. Instead, I hear someone giving me the *salam*. I reciprocate callously. Is it just a habit or manifestation of the culture that I embrace? I smile cynically.

I browse the books on the shelves. There are many philosophical and spiritual books on Islam. I remember devouring such books in my teens. At the ripe age of 50, I think I have had enough. I move to the poetry section and notice many collections by Mahmoud Darwish, who laments and philosophises on the plight of the displaced Palestinians beautifully. Is life under hardship beautiful? Perhaps it is so to those who have not faced sufferings. What is evident is that I do not feel that my life is beautiful in the alienation that I have created and experienced. But I have not reached the point of suffering. Or perhaps my soul is too insensitive to the predicament. Life is so strange and confusing sometimes. Or is it just me who has made it complicated under the pretext of living a more dynamic and interesting life?

I move to another section and notice the book *Knowledge and the Sacred* by Seyyed Hossein Nasr. I have been looking for that book for quite a while. Among other things, it promulgates the need to embrace life on this earth as a sacred experience that must be guarded and respected always. All knowledge that is gained by mankind should support this aim. Beside it is the book *Deliverance from Error* by Al-Ghazali. I have been searching for it a long time too to guide me on the straight path.

I look at the total price of both books: $120. I ponder for a while.

Then I take out my handphone. I respond to the earlier Whatsapp message: "90/45/1, OK?" The reply came in fast. "OK!"

I look at the price of the books again. Each costs $60. So, I cannot afford to buy any of them if I decide to visit the place. I feel disappointed and leave the bookshop. I remember that just a moment ago I did not have the desire to read such difficult books. So, what do I really want?

Where is my destination?

I approach the Malay Art Gallery across the street. Perhaps there are some heritage pieces that will catch my eye. I have delved into the magical world of *kerises* about three years ago. I now own more than 50 pieces of them which come from all over the world. There are many collectors of these antique weapons in the USA, Britain, the Netherlands, France, Germany, Austria and Australia, who have brought these heritage pieces from the Nusantara region to their respective countries. My small effort is bringing them back to their homeland.

However, some doubt still lingers in my heart as to whether by collecting them I would have really preserved my cultural heritage. Is it just a hobby that will disappear when I am gone? None of my children are interested to own them. Also, have I really emboldened my identity as a Malay by doing so? Is life just a hoarding of material things and experiences in this short stay on earth? *To Have or To Be*, that is the title of a book by my favourite author, Erich Fromm.

"It's been a while," the owner exclaims.

"I haven't the means to own a new piece."

"No problem. If you like one, I can reserve it for you. I have some new *kerises* and *sundangs* that I've brought from Riau."

"*Sundang?*" My eyes open wide.

"Yes, let's go upstairs."

We adjourn to the second storey of the shop. I remember the amount of money in my wallet. It will not be enough to buy an ordinary *keris*, what more an antique *sundang*.

He takes out a *sundang* from a cabinet and passes it to me. I am immediately captivated by it. The 75-centimetre heritage piece is indeed special.

"Absolutely gorgeous," I exclaim as I look closely at its silver hilt. "Can I see the blade?"

"Be my guest."

By saying 'bismillah', I draw out the blade carefully. My chest expands upon sensing the aura of the heritage *sundang*. I ask myself as to whether the 'bismillah' is a reflection of my religious habit or my cultural identity? Is it a combination of the aim, image and action of both that has been tied to my life thus far? Is character an embodiment of shapes of time that have been carved onto our feelings, thoughts and deeds; shapes of times that must be guarded with care and will be deformed by inappropriate, callous, disrespectful, stupid and desperate actions?

"How much is it?"

"This piece is rare. For you, my friend, $750," he says with a smile.

A reasonable price, I think. I return the smile as I realise that I cannot afford it at the moment.

"If you would like to own it, you can put down a deposit first."

I am tempted by his offer but am ashamed to offer $120 as a deposit. Sellers would normally demand more than half the price.

"I'm sorry. Not this time."

"No worries. But many have registered their interest in it."

I smile again. Bargaining depends on affordability, after all; affordability to accept or reject whispers of desires materially or spiritually.

My handphone vibrates. I read the message on the screen: "Coming, babe?"

My mind's focus is disturbed momentarily. I shake the owner's hand and leave the shop.

"Address?" I send a message.

"Aliwal Park Hotel."

"That's near," I say to myself. "90/45/1, right?"

"Yes, babe. Are you coming?"

My body trembles and I am breathless. My hand is shaking when I type "Yes."

"OK, babe, let me know when you have arrived. See you," she responds.

I walk slowly but desperately to the destination. The bargaining resumes in my soul again. I have the means to entertain my desire. The question is whether I would gain or lose from it.

Arriving at Aliwal Street, I scan the surroundings. Nobody I know is there. I send another message. "I have reached."

"OK, babe, my room number is 322."

I enter the hotel lobby and walk straight to the lift. The receptionist at the desk just observes me without any discernible reaction. Perhaps she is used to such antics by visitors like me.

Arriving on the third floor, I go straight to room 322 and knock on the door which opens slowly.

"*Sawadikaap*," she says gently with a smile.

I observe her sexy body. My chest trembles as it expands in heat. She pulls my hand and closes the door.

She asks me to sit on the bed. Then she signals to ask for payment.

I give her $100. She returns $10 to me.

"OK, babe, 45 minutes and 1 shot, yeah!" She then undresses herself. I pounce on her greedily.

After wrestling with our lusts for half an hour, I blast all the meanings of religion, knowledge and culture that I have accumulated all these years into her wet and sticky vagina. It is bizarre, extreme! My moral worth is wasted in the desperate and pleasurable ejaculation.

When we have finished, we bathe together. Then she dresses and kisses me. I return the kiss as a gesture of appreciation before I leave. There isn't any palpitation in my chest, only fatigue and emptiness.

I do not use the lift but the staircase. I exit through the fire door at the back of the building. My soul has been gutted by sin. I look around. Nobody has seen me. I feel relieved.

I head towards North Bridge Road with the intention to return home. I look at my watch. It is near *maghrib* or dusk prayer time. I cross the road. Reaching the other side, I stop and stand still for some time.

What have I done? And what made me conclude that nobody has seen me? God and the angels Munkar and Nakir have surely witnessed my indiscretion. How did I end up adulterating my soul with such despicable behaviour?

I sigh. A heap of regret hit my chest that is now congested and dark. I close my eyes and take a deep breath.

"*Astaghfirullah*, God forgive me!"

My entire life has plummeted into the abyss of sin within a short period. I deserve to be called a fornicator, a hypocrite!

Tears flow down my cheeks. I have to face God's wrath. Surely.

I ask myself whether my entire life would have changed if I reverse the sequence of events by indulging in sin at the hotel, then dig up cultural references at the heritage shop, and look out for knowledge at the bookshop before performing prayer at the mosque? Just a short while ago, I doubted the notion of a good ending. With the serious sin that I have committed and with whatever that is left of my life, I am now wishing for it instead.

"No worries. Allah will guide you. Just ask Him."

The parting words of the Imam reverberates in my mind. I cry and whisper a small request; just a small request because I feel shameful and remorseful.

Suddenly, I hear the *azan* or call of prayer from Sultan Mosque. Is there any opportunity for me to repent? My body and soul feel filthy. If I were to respond to His call, I have to perform the obligatory bath to cleanse my body after sex, first. Is there enough time?

Without thinking, I make my move. I turn my head to the left. I see the image of a truck that overpowers me and the shadow of an angel that crosses my path. I hear the eerie screeching of tyres on the tarmac. Then, boom!

My body flings forward. Blood splashes on the road surface. My soul departs from my body, floats and soars in the air.

Where am I heading to? In the return, my soul seems to detect the aroma of heavenly food from Bussorah Street for the last time.

"*Allahuakbar. Allahuakbar. Laailahaillallah.*"

The *azan* envelopes the dusk.

3

Glass

Kerretakk! Pianngg!

The glass panel which she knocks her head on breaks into pieces. Ana touches her forehead. It is wet. She looks at her hand. It is red.

"Ana! Don't do it! Don't knock your head on the concrete wall! Oh, God! What's happening to my daughter!"

"I want to break it! I can't bear to remain in this glass enclosure! It's suffocating!"

"What are you saying, Ana? It's not a glass panel. It's a concrete wall!"

"Shut up! Just shut up!"

"Say a prayer, Ana. Say it."

"Damn it, just shut up! I can't take it anymore. It's painful!"

Kalsum gazes at her daughter. The sadness hurts her. Her teardrops fall onto the floor.

Ana tries to stand up. She stumbles and cries in pain.

"Mum, I'm hurting. It's so painful!"

"I know Ana, I know."

While wiping her tears, she supports her daughter to the bedroom. Ana cannot walk without support. Her left leg is deformed. It has been so since the eerie incident.

Ana remembers when her body was gliding in the air. Her head had felt heavy as if all the blood cells in her body had gathered there, pushing and pushing, demanding to spurt out.

Kerretakk! Pianngg!

The blood did gush out, splattered all over the broken glass pieces when her body had landed on the roof of a car that was parked under the 15-storey building. Then she felt as if her body was pierced all over. She was gasping for air.

"Ana! Ana!"

"It's painful, Mum! So painful! I'm afraid, Mum, so afraid!"

"Please, Ana. Don't think about the incident anymore. I'm here. I'll take care of you."

Kalsum utters those words in regret. She did not fulfil her responsibilities then. She regretted not giving Ana the love and attention she deserved.

She had been too engrossed with her career, attending conferences and seminars all the time. As a professional, she had to prove her capability at work.

There was no glass ceiling that could prevent her from achieving her goals, including her marriages. Twice she had tried to build a family but both attempts had collapsed. Sometimes she regretted marrying.

Her quest for excellence had influenced the way she brought up her daughter. She remembered how she had scolded and punished her for failing to get top marks in her examinations. There was no reason that Ana could not be the best student. Ana was then prevented from leaving her room whilst her friends were celebrating their success.

Since her divorce from her two husbands, Kalsum felt that she had to manage her daughter who was a teenager then. She restricted her social circle. In fact, she managed everything about her daughter's life like she was organising the agendas of her meetings.

"Mum, please help me! I can't breathe!"

Ana's screams woke her up from her daydream. She saw Ana's chest palpitating heavily. She was gasping for air.

"Oh, God! What should I do?" She gets overwrought.

She was overwrought when she had an argument with her first husband, who accused her of cheating on him. But she was attending a meeting, just a meeting.

She was also overwrought when Ana's stepfather was in bed with a woman in her bedroom. Yes, in her own bedroom. But she did not see who that woman was. Actually, she did not want to know. She was too angry and disappointed that she ran out of the house in a hurry.

But she did not realise that her daughter was more devastated than her at that moment.

"Mum, please bring me home. I want to go home."

"You're at home, Ana. You aren't in the hospital."

"You're lying. That's the doctor, the police! They're here to restrict me in this glass enclosure!"

"You're in your own room, Ana. Not in the ICU."

"You're lying, lying!"

Ana felt claustrophobic. Everyone who was outside the enclosure was chiding her, who was deformed. Her leg was impaired. Her face was disfigured because she had broken her jaw.

She tried to move her hands, but they were numb. Her heart was reaching out for care and attention, but no one outside the glass enclosure noticed her. The glass panels had become a barrier between them. Its transparency had failed to let light enter their hearts.

Suddenly, a shadowy figure approached her. She trembled. Sweat appeared on her forehead. The shadowy figure carved a dirty smile on his lips. From his glances, she somewhat felt his deep loneliness.

The shadowy figure touched her arm, then her hair, cheeks and neck. Then ...

"Please don't, Uncle. Please don't! I hate it, hate it!"

Kalsum prevents Ana from knocking her head on the concrete wall again. She realises that Ana's soul is broken.

She gazes at Ana dejectedly. She seems to be so far away although sitting next to her, as if she is in another world. Her eyes tear up.

But she feels vindicated at that moment as Ana hates her stepfather whom she calls uncle, although she is not sure of the reason. But she senses something is amiss, a result of the alienation and loneliness that pervaded their marriage. It makes her feel that the vindication is empty and in fact has left an excruciating pain in her heart.

"This life is too fragile like glass." Her soul falls and breaks to pieces onto the hard and painful surface of reality.

"Mum, my chest is tight. My throat is dry. Can you get me some water, please?"

Kalsum is surprised that Ana has turned calm. "Yes, Ana. Just a moment. I'll get it."

Kalsum walks to the kitchen, but her steps are heavy and her heart is pounding strongly.

As soon as her mother has left the room, Ana drags her body on the bed closer to the window. She opens it and the cold air caresses her cheeks. She feels her chest expanding as she scans the wide sky. Her leg no longer feels the pain, her body feels light.

Amidst the white clouds, she feels like a bird; a bird with wings that have recovered from injury; a bird that is free to glide in the sky; a bird that has escaped the glass cage.

Kerretakk! Pianngg!

The glass in Kalsum's hand drops onto the floor. Her eyes look at the window which is open. Ana is gone.

4

Green Man Plus

He sits on a bench and watches children chasing each other and frolicking at the playground a few metres away. He smiles. He still remembers his childhood days at the kampong. The entire kampong and the nearby hill were his playground. It felt good to be free and cheerful.

He looks up at the sky. It is blue everywhere. There is not a single cloud to be seen. It is a lovely day to be out in the open and feeling alive. But he is in no mood to relish the moment. He sighs deeply. He looks at the children again. His eyes become teary.

Just a few minutes ago he had been at the hospital. The doctor told him the bad news. He has a tumour in his large intestines.

He keeps wondering. He has been living a healthy lifestyle. He exercises almost every day. Only rain keeps him away from brisk walking and doing some stretching at the park. He eats a balanced diet of carbohydrate, protein and greens. He has no major worries as he enjoys his retirement days. How did the tumour arise?

The doctor told him that he needed to undergo a biopsy soon. The tumour has grown to the size of a golf ball. If it is malignant and grows bigger and bursts, then the problem might spread to other parts of his body and it would be hard to control the disease.

He breathes in deeply and shuts his eyes. He must not worry too much. The doctor told him that the 'problem' was still manageable. He was advised to remove the tumour regardless of the outcome of the biopsy. As such, the doctor suggested that both procedures be done in one surgical operation and he had arranged it for next Monday.

He opens his eyes and places his palms on his thighs. He looks at the surface of the bare ground. An eerie thought shakes his usually calm disposition. He cannot help but imagines himself underground six feet deep. He trembles.

"Arre you reaady to crosss ooverrr?"

A guttural voice suddenly shakes the branches of the trees swayed by a gush of wind. A flock of crows takes flight. Where did they come from? His face turns pale. He panics and turns his head around. There is nobody to be seen. Even the playground is now empty. A frightful memory which creaks and pendulates with the empty swing seizes him.

Two months ago, at the religious class at the mosque, the *ustaz* told his followers that a person would be able to know of the coming of his or her death a hundred days before the event. God will reveal the signs to His servants who have been performing all the religious obligations. It is a privilege since death is a moment of celebration for the soul to return willingly to the Creator in a tranquil and contented state. This state is known as *husnul khatimah* or the 'best of ends'. As such, the coming of death should not be feared.

Everything was as usual after the class. He left for his home by walking slowly along the footpath from the mosque after the *asar* prayers. The din from the nearby coffee shop could be heard on the warm but breezy afternoon. His mind and soul felt enlightened and peaceful. That was before he experienced it.

Just as he reached a nearby bench, he suddenly felt a spasm that ran from his head to his arms and right down to his thighs and feet. The spasm shook him terribly and he had to hold onto the armrest firmly before he sat down on the bench. His chest heaved heavily and his whole body trembled. Cold sweat appeared on his forehead and nape.

His body felt numb after the spasm ended. His mind went blank for a moment. His face turned white as he realised the significance of the experience. That was the first sign! Was it? He was dazed for a while. He had never felt so lost and fearful in his entire life.

The *ustaz* had reassured his followers that the discernment of the approach of death would leave the faithful servant calm and humble as he or she prepared for the moment of release and glory. The initial bewilderment would change into complete surrender as the signs are unfolded to the servant one by one. Naturally, the servant would be doing all the things in the remaining days that would be important or meaningful to be left behind for his or her loved ones. But he or she would be accomplishing these with a state of mind of someone who knew of and cherished the manifestation of the big secret between God and His faithful servant alone. Just as the *ustaz* had said, it would be an honour or privilege.

But it had not felt like an honour or privilege as he dragged his feet to return home that afternoon. He was sullen and dazed. His body shook as he prepared to go to sleep. At an instance, he was afraid that he might wake up in a grave the next morning. But he remembered that if the sign was true, then he would have another 99 days to live. As such, he should not feel threatened by sudden death. Yet, to anticipate death was just so terrible. He did not have his dinner or sleep that night. He told himself to be on the lookout for the next sign.

The second sign would appear 40 days before the fateful day. Anxious of his possible demise, for the last two months or so he had been performing all the *wajib* or obligatory religious duties. He also performed the *sunnat* or additional duties to gain the pleasure of Allah.

Gradually, he became at peace with himself. He forgot about all his anxieties until three days ago.

The fateful second sign came after the *asar* prayer again. As he was sitting cross-legged and resting his back against one of the pillars in the mosque, he felt an excruciating pain at his navel that would not go away. He held his stomach and bent his body forward and backward repeatedly to ease the pain. He could not help but cried. That was when one of the members of the congregation noticed his suffering and approached him. He was kind enough to send him to the Accident and Emergency section of the Changi General Hospital.

He was then warded for treatment and examination. The tumour was eventually discovered. He felt restless and afraid staying at the hospital. He pleaded incessantly to the doctor to let him return home. He was finally given home-leave over the weekend, since none of the operating theatres were available and the pain in his stomach had disappeared after he was given painkillers. But he was advised by the doctor to rush to the hospital as soon as he felt the pain again. In any case, he had to return for the surgery. He promised to do so. He just wanted to spend more time at home. He had a lot to think about.

According to the *ustaz*, 40 days before death, the leaf in which the name of the servant had been inscribed since his creation would fall from the Lote Tree in Heaven. The Angel of Death would then follow the person everywhere, in preparation for his duty to snatch or pull out the life-force from the person's body. Sometimes he would appear in person to forewarn him or her. Upon seeing the Angel of Death, the person would naturally be confused for a moment until he or she realised the significance of the visit.

He shudders while holding on to the thought. He looks straight into the distance. He feels as if he is being sucked into a time tunnel. He is almost breathless.

Suddenly, he sees a man in black robe standing in front of him about 50 metres away. He is smiling wickedly at him. He can feel his over-powering presence. His lips begin to move.

"Arre you reaady to crosss ooverrr?"

That eerie voice reverberates again. Each syllable seems to pound on his eardrums. He cups his ears with his palms. He looks straight into the eyes of the stranger. They are large and hollow.

His face turns white. Goose pimples appear on his arms and cheeks. He shuts his eyes. His body shakes uncontrollably.

He tightens his eyelids for some time. He waits until the chatter of his teeth abates. Then he opens his eyes slowly. He scans the surroundings with the anticipation of shutting his eyes again. Fortunately, the man or whoever he might have been is no longer around.

He feels relieved momentarily. A deadening silence hovers in the air. His body starts to tremble again as soon as the memory of the man in the black robe attacks him again.

Dusk is approaching. He decides to return home.

He needs to hop on a feeder bus that will bring him to the bus stop nearest to his flat. He takes out his purple senior citizen concession card. Now that he is above 60 years old, he is entitled to the privileges associated with the concession card. His travel by bus and MRT train is cheaper and he gets discounts while shopping at NTUC FairPrice supermarkets every Tuesday. He gets to see movies at certain theatres at a discounted ticket price, too.

The government has also taken initial steps to implement several measures to enable the establishment of the 'ageing-in-place' lifestyle in the housing estates and at transport nodes. These steps are being taken in anticipation of the increase in the number of elderly citizens in the near future.

A small but significant measure taken by the Land Transport Authority is the introduction of the 'Green Man Plus' scheme which allows the elderly to cross the road safely and comfortably at selected pedestrian crossings. A device has been fitted at the traffic light post which prolongs the duration of crossing upon request. All the elderly needs to do is to tap the purple card at the device and the Green Man of the traffic light will blink for an additional six seconds. One such scheme was recently implemented at the pedestrian crossing near his flat. He has been using it every day since and is grateful that he need not rush to cross the road. Alas! He has not many more days left to enjoy such privileges.

He is deep in thought as he boards the bus that will take him home. If the signs were true, he would be dead in less than 40 days. The third sign would appear seven days before the tragic day. This would only be experienced by those who are ill. He realises that he may fall into that category if the tumour bursts or the impending surgery fails. He is gripped by fear. The sign would be that a person who had lost his appetite due to illness would suddenly relish food like never before. He dreads such an experience. He does not want to enjoy food just to die a few days later.

The fourth sign would surface just three days before death, after the *asar* prayer too. He would feel pain in the middle of his forehead. The light in his pupils would fade, his nose would sink in and this could be noticed from his side profile. His earlobes would wilt and the edges would curl in. His feet would also bend inwards so much so that it would be unstable for him to stand stationary for too long. It would be best that he performs the fast during the remaining days. This would ensure that his stomach and intestines would not be filled with too much excrement during the washing of the body upon death.

The final sign would appear just one day before the return to his Lord. He would feel a pulsating pain at the top of his head on a spot known as the *ubun-ubun*. If that sign were to appear, it would mean that he would not get to meet the next *asar* prayer. There would be no turning back. He would definitely meet his Creator.

His eyes are teary as he alights from the bus and walks listlessly towards the pedestrian crossing. The Green Man has not appeared. He takes out the purple card and taps it onto the 'Green Man Plus' device with his trembling hand.

"Am I ready to cross over?"

An eerie feeling suddenly overwhelms him. He feels the presence of the man with the black robe again. He looks everywhere but the apparition is nowhere to be seen. But somehow, he feels that he is being trailed and watched. He shuts his eyes in the hope that he could dispel the fear of meeting him again.

Suddenly, a hopeful and rather devious thought crosses his mind. He is struck by its simplicity and promise.

If he could add six seconds to the duration of his crossing, perhaps he could incrementally do the same to his life. It is an outrageous proposal but he does not think it is impossible. No, not at all! In fact, he is desperately hopeful about it. After all, he has nothing to lose and more time to gain. Yes, more time! He could beat the apparition at his own game and chase him away!

Something within him breaks. He laughs heartily. He is not afraid anymore. He then grins unabashedly. He waves the purple card victoriously.

As the Green Man appears, he crosses the road briskly and waits at the other end for the Red Man to appear next. When it does, he taps his purple card again to wait for the Green Man to re-appear and add six seconds to his life as he re-crosses the road. He repeats the procedure with a confident and cunning smile.

At first, nobody notices his antics. After a while, the motorists become frustrated because the traffic lights at the crossing turn red more often and they have to wait an additional six seconds each time the crazy old man crosses the road.

But nobody can stop him. He has not broken any law. All they can do is to sneer and shout at him. Some motorists avoid the crossing and make a detour. Many passers-by just gather and observe the old man who never stops grinning as he waves and taps his purple senior citizen concession card at the 'Green Man Plus' device that has given him hope of an extended crossover.

Amidst the spectacle, nobody seems to notice a van which suddenly stops near the traffic light control box by the side of the road. A man in black overalls steps out from the van. He is holding a pair of pliers.

5

Otai

He is feeling unsettled. The congregation members are just leaving the courtyard of the Sultan Mosque when he arrives in Muscat Street. A few years ago, the street had been transformed by the erection of gateways, murals and carvings, telling tourists of the history and influence of the Hadramaut community who had brought Islam to this region. Kampong Glam used to be called Kampong Haji. Sighing, he tries to imagine the chaotic bargaining that must have taken place between the prospective pilgrims to Mecca and the merchants.

Things would have been very lively at that time, although in a somewhat cautious way, because the main item on sale was the opportunity to fulfil one of the greatest commands of the Muslim religion. Now, there are only the worshippers, a few visitors including the tourists, and a row of motorcycles parked on the ornamental granite strips in the area outside the mosque. Malays had lived and traded here ever since the arrival of Raffles. Other groups – Indians, Chinese and Arabs – had prospered and enlivened the area as well. At the beginning of the 1990s, the government took over the area and transformed it in order to encourage tourism.

Bussorah Street has a religious bookshop called Wardah, the Malay Art Gallery, some souvenir shops, and restaurants selling local and foreign food. Around the corner in nearby Arab Street, merchants still sell mass-produced sarongs in various patterns. The shophouses in Haji Lane have been fitted out with pubs and various other forms of entertainment and art directed at young people. Kampong Glam is at its liveliest once the sun has set.

He sits on a granite bench and looks around. A young man in a white skullcap approaches him, holding out a pamphlet. "Help us please, brother," the young man says. He smiles. After the youth has left him, he flicks through the pamphlet. It is written in support of a proposal to free Kampong Glam from shops that sell alcoholic beverages.

For a moment, he is lost in thought. From where he sits, the minarets look slanted. He sighs. Then he looks at his watch and sighs again. He is waiting for a friend. The friend had introduced him to the world of the *keris*, the Malay dagger.

They had first met at the Malay Art Gallery. He had only intended to look around the handicraft shop. The young man was examining an old *keris*. He was attracted to the weapon as well. Unexpectedly, the young man handed him the dagger. He was flustered. He had never held a *keris* before. From what he knew, the *keris* was a classical heirloom and full of magical power. One needed to treat it with great caution and respect. At first, he was reluctant to hold the weapon. After the young man encouraged him a little, he finally plucked up courage and took the dagger by its finely carved hilt.

"A *tajong keris* from Kelantan," the young man said briefly. For some reason, just holding the dagger made him feel brave and important.

"A *keris* fit for an aristocrat," the youth continued. He smiled. It wasn't clear whether the young man was flattering him or whether he did really look distinguished. Whatever the case, he felt proud and somehow special. Their friendship began after he had bought the *keris*.

"In the world of *keris*, we don't 'buy' a *keris*," the young man said seriously. "We 'offer a dowry' for it. It is a sign of respect for this national heritage."

The more he came to know the young man, the more respect he felt for his knowledge of the world of the *keris*. The young man knew how to distinguish between a traditional and authentic *keris* and the many ornamental *kerises* offered for sale in the cyber world of eBay, Facebook and the webpages of antique merchants. He owned many well-made and valuable weapons. In the world of the *keris*, he was respectfully known as *otai*, a venerable expert.

As he was a novice in this world, he had taken the opportunity to learn from the webpages of the Southeast Asian Archipelago Classical Keris Academy and Keris Collectors Online, with an open mind, so that he might know more. He gradually came to understand terms such as *hulu* (the hilt), *bilah* (the blade), *luk* (the curves on the blade), *ganjar* (the neck of the blade), *puting* (the piece of the blade which fits into the hilt), *kerawang* (the lace fretwork decorations), *pamor* (the damascene patterns on the blade), *pendokok* (the metal ring at the base of the hilt), *pendok* (the metal casing for the lower stem of the sheath), *sampir* (the cross piece of the sheath), *serunai* (the middle part of a wooden sheath) and so on.

This was an exciting and attractive world. In fact, he started to accumulate *kerises*. Within six months, he had acquired nine *kerises* from various parts of the archipelago. With his new knowledge, he was beginning to know the different features of *kerises* from different areas. He had begun to know the difference between a new *keris* and an antique damascened *keris* which always required a higher dowry.

There were many tricks to make a new *keris* appear like an antique damascened *keris* once it has been cast. He always consulted with an *otai* in such matters so that he had the best advice possible before seeking to 'marry' a *keris*. Apart from acquiring *kerises*, he had begun to gather other accessories such as headcloths, waist sashes, knee length sarongs, belts and waist buckles, to complete the traditional Malay clothing he owned.

He started learning about the history, philosophy and aesthetics of *keris* manufacture so that his understanding went beyond merely technical details. His aim was to become a true Malay fit for a modern nation. The attempt to connect the modern and the traditional planted the seeds of discord between himself and the *otai*.

"How can we defend our heritage if we are unfaithful to the ancient ways of making a *keris*?" the *keris* master demanded.

"But we are living in a modern world," he replied. "We need to change the way we make a *keris*."

"Many so-called developments have only one purpose: to attract customers and, in particular, tourists," the *otai* added. "They don't follow the old ways. They might seem beautiful, but they are only frivolous ornamentation."

"Not all of these features are ornaments," he replied. "Some craftsmen have experimented with a combination of modern features and other traditions from throughout the Malay world."

"For example?"

"What is wrong with combining a Javanese blade with a Buginese sheath, in a way that recognises the latest fashions?"

"That's impossible," his colleague replied. "Each region has its own characteristic features. You can't just add a contemporary touch. That sort of *keris* would be purely ornamental."

"But our contemporary Malay identity is already a mixture of various ethnic identities. And we've absorbed some of the values of modern life as well. Why shouldn't we do the same when we make *kerises*?"

"Only a newcomer to the world of *kerises* would think that way," the master snapped. "He knows very little, yet he feels qualified to challenge those who have studied these matters deeply. It takes a qualified jeweller to appreciate a diamond."

"That's true," he replied with a sneer. "It takes a qualified jeweller to appreciate a diamond. The problem is that some jewellers only know about diamonds and nothing else."

Once the discussion reached this point, they always left it hanging. Each had his own way of restraint so as not to destroy their relationship. And they had arranged to meet that afternoon to deal with a similar problem. They had decided to meet in order to discuss the *Rangsang Rias Keris* Festival that was soon to be staged in the renovated Kampong Glam palace. The annual programme was open to local and foreign enthusiasts as a means of promoting the *keris* and its world. There were displays of *kerises*, martial arts performances, ritual *keris* purification bathing ceremonies and lectures about the weapon. The aim was to teach the public about the traditional heritage of the *keris* and the cultural aspects that were related to it.

As usual, his friend insisted that the various presentations should only focus on the traditional aspects of the *keris* world while he himself was in favour of the renewal of the old ways.

"Have you been waiting long?" The voice interrupts his musing. He stands up and shakes hands with the *keris* master.

"I could wait forever for the world to change," he replied impudently. The master responds to the remark with a loud laugh.

"Come on," the *otai* invites, once he has stopped laughing, "let's go and have a drink."

They turn and enter Bussorah Street. The street is lined with palm trees. Several men pass them, dressed in long gowns and turbans. The master stops walking and watches the different groups as they enter the mosque grounds.

"Look at that!" he snarls. "They are Malays, but they're dressed in gowns and turbans like Arabs. Obviously, they have no respect for their own culture. They call themselves Malays, but they're not!"

"They're dressed modestly, as religion requires," he replies.

"What is wrong with wearing Malay clothing? It is modest too, and it preserves our cultural heritage. Look at me."

He suddenly realises that his friend is dressed in a Malay-style shirt and sarong. Perhaps, because he is so used to the costume, he no longer appreciates its unique qualities. The master is wise to preserve his traditional Malay culture in this way. They may have disagreed on many other matters, but he respects the master's absolute determination and sincerity in refusing to give a single inch in this particular struggle.

"All right," he says, throwing the pamphlet into a bin. "Who cares? I'm hungry ... The usual place?"

"Let's go!" his friend replies. They go to a café at the end of Bussorah Street that offers local and Turkish food. The waiter smiles when he sees them.

"The same as usual, boss?" asks the waiter.

"The same drinks as usual ..." he responds, turning to his friend. "What would you like to eat?"

"I'll try fusion today," answers his friend.

He laughs. "I thought you only ate Malay food."

"I like to try something else from time to time," the master remarks, laughing. "It's boring eating the same thing every day."

"Fine. I'll have fried noodles. And you?"

"I'll have shish kebab with black soy sauce," says the master.

"The same as usual to drink, boss?" the waiter repeats.

"Of course, the same as usual!" the master replies, annoyed.

The waiter retreats to the kitchen to protect himself from further attack. It is becoming darker. The shops begin switching on their lights. A few young men in skullcaps and women wearing veils leave the Wardah bookshop and hurry towards the mosque. A few minutes later, the twilight call to prayer reverberates mournfully through the evening air.

The waiter returns carrying a tray loaded with the drinks the two men have ordered. He approaches them and places both bottles on the table.

The *otai* reaches for the opened bottle and examines it eagerly, as if it were a special *keris*. As he raises his glass, he shouts delightedly, "Cheers!"

"Cheers!" he replies, clinking his glass against that of the master's. The beer froths in their glasses. They contentedly gulp down their Carlsbergs.

"Aaaah!"

The call to prayer continues to ring out from the Sultan Mosque.

6

The Gardener

Regret was an unsuitable word to describe his feelings because regret would mean that he was the guilty party. Rather, he was dismayed – a dismay which has shaken his status as a successful individual.

What was the worth of the wilting jasmine plant at the edge of the driveway? Perhaps it was only several dollars. It could be replaced at any time and bought from anywhere.

But for him, the jasmine plant was his entire life. It could not be replaced or bought easily. He heaved a long sigh. His strength to continue with his work in the garden had dissipated. What was the purpose of loosening the soil in preparation for plants to grow if the plants were to share the fate of the jasmine? What was the point of sowing the seeds if the roots of the plants were only to be scattered?

His thoughts were interrupted by the sound of a vehicle. A car passed in front of his garden. Its wheels crushed the petals of the withered jasmine.

Like one who was threatened with destruction, he jumped immediately onto the edge of the driveway and picked up the remains of the jasmine. Now, his entire life history has been shattered. No one would appreciate his efforts.

His weary eyes became wet. The drops of tears rolling down his cheeks could not bring those leaves and flowers back to life.

He remembered the moment when he had presented the jasmine to his beloved wife. She had requested it to be planted in the garden. As a symbol of love, she said. He recollected the traumatic moments before his wife breathed her last. Her sad voice rang in his ear, "Dear, take good care of our child. Provide him with a good education. Take care of him as you would the jasmine plant. When he has grown up, show him the jasmine his mother loved."

Since the death of his wife after the delivery of their only child, he took good care of both his child and the plant. In his heart, they were his most valuable possessions.

As a gardener, he realised that he could not provide his son with riches. Being illiterate, he did not have the capacity to educate his son. Fortunately, there were teachers in the school who could fulfil that role.

Unlike the times when he was young, this modern era was endowed with many opportunities and facilities. It was not difficult for a person with talents to develop them. All it took was keen interest and unyielding efforts.

With a strong determination, he had aspired to mould his child into an intelligent person. He had hoped to send him to the university in line with the aspiration of his late wife.

He remembered the times when they cycled to school in the mornings. Upon returning, he would attend to his garden at once. The jasmine plant which he dearly loved would be watered. Sometimes, he would nourish the plant with compost. Any weeds growing nearby would be removed. Any pest around would be thrown far away from the plant he loved. Such meticulous care was taken and the plant grew well.

The plant not only symbolised his love for his late wife and it did not only represent the flowering of his hopes for his son's future, but the plant also embodied the meaning of his relationship with nature and God.

The meaning of this relationship became more significant when his son left to further his studies abroad. His life, which had become lonely, made him ponder over matters a great deal. He realised more than ever that his daydreams would not be as deep as the reflections of his son who had received higher education. His understanding of matters was simple, and far from the complicated ideas discussed in the lectures attended by his son.

At times he was even envious of his son. If only he had been born in this modern age, the opportunities to develop his intellect would certainly have been enhanced. The extent of knowledge and the ease with which such knowledge could be taught would surely have enabled him to live a more meaningful life.

But his world was only the garden. Through his plants, such as the jasmine, he felt a gentle closeness with nature. Each drop of perspiration from his gardening produced a robust and healthy life. It was as if his love for nature was continuously returned.

The unending peace in the garden gave him a sense of satisfaction with life. However, this satisfaction did not make him forget himself. He realised even more that the satisfaction he felt was a gift from God.

He knew that he was not the one who caused the leaves to grow. Nor was he the one who provided these flowers with scent. He realised that he was only a human being who was endowed with a sensitive heart and a willing body.

If only he could grasp the process of growth which had taken place in plants such as the jasmine, certainly his understanding would be more refined and beautiful. Surely his love for nature would be enhanced and gratitude towards God be deepened. But he was merely a gardener who did not understand all these complicated things.

At times, he was disappointed at his own limitations. However, such dejection would give way to joy when he realised that his son would certainly be able to fathom all these matters. "So fortunate is my child," he often remarked.

But his smiles faded and was replaced by sighs which had forced their way into his innermost feelings. Only the remains of his jasmine plant were left. The plant which he loved had become a victim. Without his knowledge, it had been cut down because it was regarded as an obstruction to a car – the car which was driven by his own son, his son who had returned home with a degree.

Instantly, his soul revolted. His daydreams were overwhelmed by exasperation. He gripped the earth and clenched the soil firmly. He hurried to the side of his house to fetch his old bicycle.

He rode speedily towards the school where his son had once studied. The questions haunting his mind demanded just and immediate answers. Surely there would be teachers able to explain all of these. "Surely!" his soul screamed.

7

The Clinic

"Who's unwell?"

The question pierces his eardrums. A nurse tries to verify which of the persons in front of her is really ill.

It is indeed true that verification is needed in life. Without it, there would be confusion in the mind and emptiness in the heart.

These thoughts linger in his mind. His presence at the clinic is also to verify whether he is ill. If so, what is the remedy?

Sixty-five. That is the waiting number assigned to him. He has to wait for his turn as part of the rules. Without adherence to rules, there would not be propriety. Every human being should abide by rules. "Unlike that rude young man!" exclaims Pak Seru, while stroking his numb left arm.

That arm became numb a week ago when he was shaken by an argument with the young man.

Is it possible that a disturbance in the soul could affect the physical self? Why not! He believes in the unseen world.

But why is he at the clinic to seek verification? Ah! Because he believes that there is a human being more knowledgeable in matters of health. That human being is called a doctor. Believing in the expertise of the doctor is also part of propriety.

"Pak Seru, do you believe that the external world could affect the internal world?" That question reverberates in his ears.

"We must live like a fish which swims in salty water, but its body isn't salty."

"But human beings aren't fish. We've thoughts and feelings which are affected by the surroundings."

"Ah, that isn't important, as long as we've strong faith!"

"But would faith alone protect us from danger and filth because our character is formed by the social, economic and political environment, whether we're aware or not?"

"Up to what level is your religious education?" It was easy for Pak Seru to block his arguments. Now he smiles at his victory.

"Twenty-five," the nurse calls a patient. The smell of medicine enters his nostrils. Verily, he does not like the smell of medicine.

"Pak Seru, why don't you look at what has afflicted our village youths?"

"What has happened?"

"How many of them are in the drug rehabilitation centre? How many girls have fallen into prostitution? How many of our youths are unemployed while people like you are still doing the same thing?"

"That isn't my fault. My job is to convey the message."

"I'm not blaming you, Pak Seru. I just want to discuss it with you. Perhaps all your efforts fall short of its real aim."

"Thirty-five." A man rises from his seat and walks towards the nurse.

"Please enter the room. The doctor will give you an injection."

Injection! Pak Seru becomes nervous.

"Haven't you noticed those problems arose when our lives in the village transformed gradually to that of an industrial city? When our perceptions of life became muddled and confused from the barrage of technological developments?"

"That's none of my business. I'm a religious teacher."

"I don't deny your role. But perhaps the way you convey religion is inadequate."

"Up to what level is your religious education?"

He recollected how he had thwarted the young man's arguments earlier. But this time, he is not smiling.

The smell of medicine makes him nauseous. The threat of an injection is chilling to his bones. He realises that he has to take them sooner or later.

"Fifty." Another patient goes in to see the doctor. One by one, the patients in the clinic receives treatment. Each has his or her own ailment. Nowadays, it seems that there are many new illnesses that have never appeared before. This is part of the reality of the times that cannot be denied.

"Perhaps the young man is right. Maybe his efforts are inadequate."

His chest expands suddenly. His left arm which had felt heavy now seems lighter.

"Sixty-five!" Now it is his turn to see the doctor. His time of reckoning has arrived. He will certainly know of his illness. He wants to receive treatment fast. He wants to be well again.

"That's good," exclaimed the doctor.

"What's good, doctor?" he asks while attempting to look at the doctor's face. A bright light is directed at his eyes that makes the doctor's face appear as a silhouette.

"It's good that you want to recover from the illness quickly."

Pak Seru becomes pale. How does the doctor know what is in his heart? But what perturbs him more is that he seems to recognise the doctor's voice. Who is he?

He tries to identify his face but only his smiles greet him.

"The physical and spiritual worlds exist in unity. It's only humans who separate them."

Pak Seru is terrified. The doctor knows his thoughts' history.

"Don't be afraid. Keep calm. I'll try to cure your illness. I know you very well."

"What's my illness, doctor?"

"I'll explain slowly. You must listen carefully."

"Alright. I'll listen, doctor. I'll listen attentively like a student."

"That's good. Actually, your illness arises from the heart. I'm sure you know what I mean by the heart."

"Yes, I know, doctor."

"I'd like to repeat the lesson. It's important."

"I've memorised many books that discuss the topic of the heart. You needn't explain it further. I'm actually unwell."

"Yes, I know you're unwell. But I must continue with the explanation. My role is to convey the message."

"But what you're conveying has nothing to do with my illness!"

"Isn't what I convey good?"

"That's true, doctor. But I don't require a lecture. I need medication!"

"Society also needs medication."

Pak Seru is taken aback. His eyes are focused on the silhouette in front of him.

"Now look at me carefully, Seru. You'd recognise who I am, surely."

Pak Seru's heart pounded strongly. He is curious and nervous. Who is he?

"Oh, Allah!" shouts Pak Seru. The doctor's face shocks him. He is wearing a white gown. While smiling, the doctor administers an injection on his own left arm.

8

Door

The rooster crows, but not from the chicken coop. The shrieking is from the desk clock by the bed. Aaaah! It is morning. My body is awake but not my soul. Another day to go through.

As usual, after a bath I perform my prayers, put on office attire and descend to the lower floor of the duplex apartment to have breakfast. My wife has prepared cheese sandwich and coffee. I eat and drink without any fuss because I have expected it. But I am not complaining as long as my stomach is not empty.

I walk to my children's room, kiss their foreheads and cheeks. They wriggle a little, their slumber is disturbed, but not enough to wake them up. I smile. The usual smile.

I walk to the door. I kiss my wife's forehead and lips. She hugs me. As usual, I return the hug. She grabs and turns the door knob.

The door opens.

I walk out. I descend the stairs without looking at the steps. As usual. At the ground floor, I approach the gate. I take out the automatic key from my pocket and press the button.

The gate opens.

I walk out from the courtyard. As usual, I look up. My wife waves at me. The usual wave.

I rush to the bus stop. I take out the farecard from my wallet and stand by the edge of Telok Kurau Road. I look at my watch. As usual, at exactly 7.30am, bus number 15 arrives. I wave at the driver. He returns the wave and presses the switch.

The door opens.

I sit at my usual seat. It is strange, but nobody else would occupy the seat. The bus travels the usual route, passes the usual houses, turns around the usual junction and arrives at the usual bus stop at Eunos, near the MRT station. As usual, I press the bell and wave at the bus driver. He returns the wave again and presses the switch.

The door opens.

I alight from the bus. As usual, I rush to the MRT station entrance. I take out the farecard and tap at the machine.

The faregate opens.

Eunos is an elevated station. I ride the escalator. I hear the screeching of the steel wheels of the approaching MRT train. I rush to the platform and stand at the usual spot and watch the train stop slowly. I look at the clock that is hanging from the ceiling. As usual, exactly 7.45am. I count one, two, three.

The door opens.

I step into the train cabin that is packed like sardines. I look around, looking for familiar faces. I spot many. There are new ones, but although unfamiliar, their faces look typical.

The train glides along the viaduct. It arrives at Paya Lebar. The doors open. It arrives at Aljunied. The doors open. It arrives at Kallang. The doors open. The train dives into the dark tunnel. It rumbles inside my bleak heart. Commuters look at each other. Their faces fade in the cabin light. The train arrives at Lavender. The doors open. But it is not time for me to alight yet.

The train speeds up. What is it chasing exactly? At last, it arrives at Bugis. That is my stop. Maybe. I do not have the time to ponder. I have to step out quickly, if not I will miss my destination. I weave myself through the crowd to get close to the door. Excuse me!

The door opens.

Bugis is an underground station. I ride the escalator and arrive at the concourse. I have just emerged from the bowels of the earth but my soul feels buried. I tap the farecard at the machine once again.

The faregate opens.

I rush to the company bus. Its usual wait makes me feel rushed. I let myself be swallowed by it. As usual, it starts to move at 8.15am.

The bus heads towards Middle Road, turns into Selegie Road, enters Bukit Timah Road and travels along Kampong Java Road. Although the route is meandering, the destination is the usual Land Transport Authority. It arrives at exactly 8.30am.

The door opens.

I alight from the bus. I intend to go to my office as usual. But suddenly my stomach hurts. I remember I had hot and spicy tomyam soup last night. A treat from a friend. Not the usual, and my stomach is suffering for it now. Aaaah! What inconvenience!

I rush to the toilet. I cannot bear it anymore. My stomach muscles are wrenching tightly. My rooster is crowing loudly. I remember the shrieking of the desk clock. My anus is screaming because it cannot control the inevitable. Sweat is dripping from my eyebrows. My heart is palpitating. Arriving at the toilet, I rush to the cubicle. I kick the door open. While crouching, I undo my pants hurriedly.

Aaaah, what a relief. I realise that I am able to ponder. For quite long, actually. The usual schedule is dumped into the toilet bowl.

I am sorry.

This time, I have to close the door.

9

The Architect

He is known as an architect.

Today is supposed to be a memorable day for him. His name is supposed to be carved as a benefactor of the city. A dignitary is supposed to confer on him the honour of successfully building a skyscraper that symbolises the glory of life in an all-modern city. Every inhabitant is going to remember his service to the city. Every architect is going to feel envious of his success.

But he knows better than anyone else that the picture is a farce. He is more conscious than anybody else of the fact that the building is a symbol of pure sham. Today is the day of exposure. He is going to unmask the pretence to the public. He is going to show them how devoid of a soul of loftiness that conspicuously beautiful building is.

Moments after his success in the competition to design the building for the use of a group of professionals in the city was announced, his name was on everyone's lips. Two years later, the design has turned into reality, a reality that is against his own principle and aspiration, a reality that he actually detests.

When the competition was announced, he thought it would be a great opportunity to submit his vision of a life that he dreamed of. He envisioned an arena of life where the space and opportunity to meet in harmony and freedom could be given prominence. To realise that aim, he would rather build a village than a skyscraper.

For him, a skyscraper would only create a situation where man would be more alienated from his personality and his life.

But he knew only too well that such a design would be dumped into the wastepaper basket. Each time, his concept of the village had met with the same fate – that of ridicule – as it was considered not to be in keeping with the times.

A situation like this gave him inspiration to play a practical joke: he would in pretence begin to create a skyscraper, the ideal of modern man. All materials, equipment and systems used in this building would be modern. By doing this, he was sure his plan would be accepted by the public.

His guesses had proven correct. Indeed, the panel of judges for the competition praised his design. They said that the architect who designed the building was sensitive to the demands of modern life. But he knew better how ridiculous that assessment was.

It is true he had worked earnestly in getting that design of his ready, earnest insincerity. Each stage in the process of creation was a weird moment.

He felt a sort of excruciating alienation: alienation from his own being and from the meaning of life. But it was that sense of alienation that brought him inspiration and drove him to create. In the act of producing the work, he felt as if he had been compelled to become another person.

For two years during the building of the skyscraper, he transformed himself into a modern man. For two years, he lived as a complex man: a man who considered issues more important that awareness; a man who stressed policies rather than harmony; a man who fussed over ways and means of living but neglected life. His skyscraper is the product and symbol of a man in utter confusion.

**

"Congratulations, sir. You have succeeded."

"It isn't I who have succeeded, Hijaz. Really, it is you who have succeeded. You put up this building."

"Aren't you, sir, the architect who designed this building? I am only a clerk-of-work who follows your instructions."

"In your sincerity towards your responsibilities, it is you who have succeeded. Come! I want to see this monument of insincerity for the last time."

The two of them leave the reception hall for the lift lobby of the building.

"Look at the crack at the overhanging wall, Hijaz. This building is actually imperfect."

"I can cover the crack with cement, sir. But I'm sure people will fill up this building after its official opening. Your design is, of course, attractive. Come! Let's go up, sir. Let's see how impressive your creation is."

"Good. Let's go up. But don't use the lift. The hustle and bustle of life has drowned man in transience. I want to count these last moments with my own steps. I want to tread on eternity before I go."

"You are moving to another city after the ceremony?"

"Yes, I am going away. But there's no need for any ceremony."

The two of them begin climbing up the 35-storey building. It appears that the climb is reminding him of the unforgettable moments in his life.

**

"You have now become a stranger."

"Are you leaving me, Liza?"

"Our ways of life are no longer compatible. You are always busy. You value your work more than me."

**

"On which floor are we, Hijaz?"

"On the tenth, sir. Are you feeling tired?

"Somewhat weak. But it doesn't matter. Let me use my remaining strength to follow a man like you. You don't feel tired?"

"I'm from the village, sir. My legs are village people's legs. They remain strong."

They reach a vast hall. Each of the bare mirrored walls make it even more spacious.

**

"You're a hypocrite. I have no more respect for you!"

"You're too quick with your accusation, Arif."

"You aren't firm in your stand. You're too occupied with talking. Never have you carried out what you've talked about."

"You must understand, I'm still searching for myself."

"With that laxity in your attitude, you've already lost yourself, actually."

**

"On which floor are we, Hijaz?"

"On the 20th, sir. Sir, you look pale."

The colours of the walls that appear rather bright on the lower floors have now turned dark.

**

"Pardon me for not being able to do anything. Your cancer is now at an advanced stage."

"How much longer, doctor?"

"Three months."

**

"On which floor are we, Hijaz?"

"The 30th, sir."

"Let me climb to the top alone. You wait here. I must go through the end of this journey by myself."

"Yes, sir. I understand and respect your wish. You, sir, are the best qualified person to be first to get to the top."

"You, too, Hijaz, can be at the top. Go up when I reach the bottom."

He takes a deep breath and begins the final climb. He is resolute about carrying out his intention. Let it be that this time, he does not change his stand. Let it be that this time, he is going to turn his back on society because their sham has been incarnated in his own self.

Would society realise this? Would they accept his action as a sacrifice? Or are they going to despise him? Are they not going to care at all?

He reaches the top. The decisive moment nears. He looks over the horizon. Only the depressive cityscape.

He turns his view upwards. The expansive sky seems

to offer a free, untrammelled life. His congested chest appears to have been prised open and he asks his inner chest, Do I have the heart to do it?

In between the white clouds, he sees the reflections of an old housemaid and an old gardener. For 35 years, the couple have slogged for his well-being. Does he have the heart to disappoint them? Suddenly, drops of tears rolls down his cheeks.

"Oh, God! Forgive me for being desperate."

He goes on crying like a child. In his loneliness, he can feel how sinful it is to harbour that desire in his heart. In his realisation, he feels the whole universe reverberating and offering the totality of its soul as a companion.

A strange yearning fills his chest. He stands up from his kneeling position. He fixes his gaze on the horizon again.

Now he sees a reflection of his ideal village in a flood of twilight glow. Also reflected is his ideal community living in peace and harmony, with Liza, Arif and Hijaz looking cheerful in their midst. But where is he?

The beautiful scene fades all of a sudden. His head spins and becomes heavy. His chest becomes short-winded. He feels weak all over his body.

From the slits of his eyelids, he sees for the last time the twilight glow engulfed by darkness. He sees his ideal village vanishing, enveloped by night.

Hijaz, who has been waiting below, climbs up to join his architect.

10

The Mimbar

Year 2219.

They shot him with a laser gun. Screams reverberated in the chamber. He collapsed on the ground with a loud thud and clunk.

Every visitor at the mosque gasped in disbelief, then relief. The police immediately rushed to check on his fallen body. He was gone. The was no light in his eyes. His right hand was still holding the axe. The pungent smell of burnt wood and metal filled the air.

Everyone looked up to the structure next to the *mihrab*. The *mimbar* was severely disfigured at the base and shaft. The granite floor was littered with splintered wood.

The mosque grounds were immediately cordoned off. The police called in the authorities to collect his body. They came swiftly and transported his body in an airborne capsule for post-mortem.

Meanwhile, the police retrieved a collection of notes from his sling bag. One of them, printed on yellowish paper, had a strange story from the past.

The mosque sits atop a small hillock. From afar it looks majestic like a palace, its design befits its name which is inspired by a prominent figure in Singapore history. From the bus stop he walks slowly along a long meandering path under an overcast sky which provides some shade. The route prepares him on his journey from a temporal domain to a sacred realm.

He wonders if the same sense of reverence could be attained during a rainy day. Many congregants would have to run quite a distance for shelter or be drenched before entering the mosque. A covered linkway from the bus stop to the entrance of the mosque would do the job, but it would mar the grand vista and appearance of the edifice. He begins to question its user-friendliness. The mosque should be designed and built as a visual delight but, more importantly, to fit its purpose as a sacred and comfortable building for the congregants physically, emotionally and spiritually.

The entrance area is airy with good cross-ventilation. He feels a sense of relief, but his soul is burdened by a lingering doubt. He takes off his shoes and enter the ablution section of the mosque to cleanse parts of his body. He recites a silent prayer to keep his intentions pure and thwart any inward distraction. But his heart begins to throb in anticipation as he makes his way to the main prayer hall. He tells himself not to have any pre-notion or judgement before he sees it with his own eyes.

The moment of truth arrives. It is the strangest feeling. There it stands erect in front of his face. He gazes at its three-metre tall brown shaft, mostly hollow, but still encapsulates the form. The suggestion is just too strong. The tip almost makes him blush, not exactly pointed, but enough to suggest its power of penetration and ejaculation. He cannot believe that it is there, making a frontal and brutal assault at the congregants in this sacred space. It is just unbelievable that no one has said anything about it until he pointed to its resemblance to a phallic symbol. Perhaps many have noticed it but chosen to remain silent for some reason.

He wants to perform the supererogatory prayer, as is encouraged on entering a mosque, but he cannot make himself face it. His mind is wavering. He moves to the side and faces a blank wall instead. A few congregants notice his discomfort and start murmuring amongst themselves, but he is not bothered. He takes a deep breath and performs the two rounds of prayer, his mind not exactly at ease, but at least he is not standing, bowing and prostrating in reverence to it. He feels somewhat redeemed.

Then he sits cross-legged and observes it from the side. The shaft is actually cantilevered from the wall. The revered Mufti has proudly referred to it as the floating pulpit or mimbar *on his Facebook page. He does not see any front steps as is customary for a* mimbar *structure. Traditionally, the congregants need to witness the Imam climb up to it when salutations to the Prophet are being recited just before the sermon. He assumes that the steps in this particular case are hidden. The Imam presumably makes his entry from the back to deliver the sermon instead, a clear departure from tradition.*

His mind wanders freely. The mimbar *suddenly appears as a cobra with a vicious head, turns into a Chinese log coffin, a dugout and then a bamboo coin-collection receptacle of olden days. Some proudly say it looks futuristic, like a rocket. Its form does evoke suggestive images.*

There are three LED-lighted arches adorning the shaft, presumably to give it a sense of cutting-edge technological glory. The peak is actually layered and accentuated by three rings of LED lights too. The parapet wall of its base is elaborately decorated by an array of orchid petals, not just any orchid but the Vanda Miss Joachim, the national flower. The mosque and mimbar *are specifically designed and built to commemorate the first Malay President of Singapore, Encik Yusof Ishak. A craftsman from*

Pahang was commissioned to collaborate with the architect to come up with the unique form and special carvings of the mimbar.

He imagines that there must have been discussions between the Islamic Religious Council, MUIS, the mosque committee and the architect on how best to depict the glory of the presidential office in the mosque. The mimbar was inadvertently chosen as it is a symbol of authority. From the start, it must have been the underlying concept of its prominence and accentuated features.

Where does he begin to say everything that is wrong with the structure? As messenger and whistle-blower, he has received numerous accusations since he posted his views of it politely on the Mufti's Facebook wall. Most of the attacks were from the mosque committee members, some religious teachers and their gang. He was referred to as an attention-seeker, having a dirty mind, a trouble-maker, agitator, creating a mountain over a mole hill, just to name a few. He begins to wonder whether the strong and extreme responses that have been pelted at him are actually clear signs that he has stepped on the nerves of many, a sign that actually they know, deep in their souls, that he is right. Otherwise, why bother to character-assassinate him? He is just a concerned observer. He has been civil and rational in expressing his views.

To him, the entire team that is responsible for the design and erection of the mimbar *does not have a clue or cultural experience to notice such atrocity. Obviously, they have not travelled to places like Prambanan and Dieng Plateau in Indonesia or other temples and villages in India, Nepal and Indochina, where such images can be readily found.*

He has no qualms about everyone remembering the late president, but to commemorate him inside the main prayer hall is just mind-boggling. Congregants want to be immersed in total remembrance of Allah in His House, and not be distracted by the memory of any person or prominence of any object. And if the mimbar *is meant to glorify or worship any authority, it is solely of Allah. Is that not what a mosque is all about?* Allahuakbar. *God is Great.* Laailahaillallah. *There is no God but Allah.*

And in terms of hierarchy, the wall indicating the direction of Mecca, the mihrab, *should take precedence over the* mimbar. *In fact, at some mosques, the* mimbar *is a movable object, dragged out from the store and placed at its position only when required. But in this mosque, it is the other way around. The* mimbar *which is used only once a week during Friday prayer has been given more prominence than the* mihrab *which functions every time there is a person praying in the mosque.*

His visits to Alhambra, Isfahan and many prominent Islamic sites made him realise that Islamic aesthetics aspire towards the dissolution of form through application of geometric and arabesque patterns on surfaces and objects within a sacred space for fear of any reference to iconography, but here the mimbar *is accentuated as the centrepiece of the mosque. And what suggestive forms it conjures? He can relate it to the Trimurti Shrine in Bangkok, the temple of love that is inspired by the* lingam *and* yoni *of Hindu iconography. The frontal view of the erect shaft is just too obvious to ignore as a* lingam *and the orchid decoration at its base is suggestive of its feminine nature as a* yoni. *The three radial rings at the shaft reminds him of the* tilaka *drawn on the forehead of Hindu priests, and the three layers of light at the peak conjures the levels of existence of Mount Meru in Hindu mythology.*

Is he imagining these things? He thinks not. The truth is he is burdened by the knowledge of its indiscretion. It is not a subjective response and evaluation.

There is obvious disconnect between knowledge and practice of religion, and culture of those who are responsible for this abomination. Their minds have also been clouded by the intention and fervour to glorify the late president.

Suddenly he hears giggles. He looks up to the second floor of the mosque. He sees three ladies in their prayer gowns smile sheepishly and pointing to the mimbar.

He is in utter disbelief. A tinge of sadness pervades his heart. If he had the power and influence, he would have the ill-designed mimbar *removed. It is just too unsettling to the heart and mind. But he is just a concerned adherent of the faith.*

So be it. He has done his duty. It is time to move on. He turns his back on the indiscretion and walks away. He shall not return.

Post-mortem. The disfigured *mimbar* was repaired and restored to its old glory. The mosque was reopened to visitors once more. It was one of the remaining buildings in the land that had been preserved as heritage to commemorate the island's first president. Nobody visited the mosque to pray or to remember Him anymore.

The police still could not figure out why Unit 777 did what he did. When they looked into his memory chip, they discovered that it was implanted with the ancient book called the Quran and records of the history of the Prophet. In it was his recorded voice proclaiming the *Shahadah* to mark his conversion to Islam in front of an Imam at some point in time.

His body was sent to the Android Compositor for recycling, but his memory chip was pounded to dust.

The police have started to hunt for the Imam and his clandestine followers.

11

The Crucible

"Do you see the hole?"

"It invites me to escape."

"No, it invites us to the freedom and vastness of nature."

"How have you been subjugated so far?"

"I do not reject rules. I only choose freedom."

"You like to daydream. Your aspirations penetrate the net."

"That which grows in you, you call a fairy tale?"

"I only believe in what I see and taste."

"In this net, where do you direct your sight? Where do you place your mouth?"

"On security. On comfort."

"Aren't you afraid of the shadow of the hands?

"What else do you want? Aren't the days always bright?"

"Don't you understand the lamps are purposely switched on?"

Two silkworms wriggle from an old twig to the wilted leaves. The net which envelopes their abode casts its shadows, slicing the leaves and their bodies into small squarish cuts.

Gleggleg. Blepblep. Puppup.

"What is that sound?"

"That's the crucible. It is the hands that prepare it."

"Haven't you noticed that the sound is heard every time the lamp in a particular net is switched off?"

"You are still attached to the ancient tale. I have stated from long ago, the moth does not exist."

"Why are you escaping from truth?"

"Is it me who has been eyeing the hole?"

"What is promised of security, what is hoped from comfort, if you would see your future in darkness?"

"I am promised the silk."

"The silk?"

"Yes! The refined, soft and elegant silk."

Gleggleg. Blepblep. Puppup.

Both the silkworms lift their heads when the sound of the crucible that obliterates the peace and tranquillity is heard. Day by day, the sound becomes more violent and the atmosphere in the net more tense.

"Don't you hear that sound? It guarantees our future. It's not akin to the moth that you have not seen and will never meet. The sound proves the existence of the crucible. The crucible that will turn us all into silk."

"Haven't you ever felt that the moth is the Creator's promise to us?"

"Isn't it us who create the cocoon that will produce silk by the hands? It shows that we are capable of weaving our future by our own efforts. The promise that we ought to keep is the one we uphold with the hands."

"Since when do we make the promise with the hands?"

"Since the hands feed us. Since the hands take care of our everyday needs."

The being that is known as the hands enters the net through an opening. The two silkworms wriggle to safety under the leaves.

"Haven't you wondered if the hands are powerless? They feed the mouth sustenance to ensure their survival. Haven't you thought where the sustenance comes from?"

"Why do you hate the hands?"

"Actually, I am not perturbed. I like order. I love peace. But I am nervous of darkness."

"Does the moth that you dream of promise light?"

"Haven't you pondered why we become the cocoon? Haven't you imagined our existence after the considerable time spent in the cocoon? It is the kiss with light. The light which shines from our wings that confronts the darkness."

"Alright then. If what you say is true, can't we achieve it here in the net?"

"Impossible, because you accept the existence of the crucible. The crucible is not our way of life, although it promises silk. If we really yearn for freedom, you must realise that our wings are broken the moment we accept the softness of silk."

"So, what are you going to do?"

"I will emigrate."

"That is dangerous."

"It's a calculated risk. I am only responding to my destiny. Isn't the bounty from the Creator vast?"

"Have you decided?"

"Yes."

"Why?"

"Because I have submitted."

"To what and whom?"

"To my natural path and the Creator."

"You are hanging onto something that is unseen. Where is the guarantee of good tidings?

Gleggleg. Blepblep. Puppup.

"Listen to that sound. It is a warning and threat. It is bad news for you."

"That sound guarantees my future. The silk is more real and beautiful than all your dreams."

"You are mistaken my friend. This net is a trap. The crucible will kill you. Are you confident that you will be living the life of silk?"

"It is as if you are not accepting the condition that we are in. Aren't we born in this net?"

"Don't you believe the narrative that those who came before us once lived in a beautiful garden? Don't you believe that they were inheritors of freedom and joy?"

"The environment has changed, my friend. You speak of the essence that does not exist now."

"It is true that it does not exist, because you think it does not. Come, my friend. Join me. Let's leave this guarded place! Free our body and mind! Let's emigrate!"

"If I were to follow you, I would leave the prosperity of this place. I would starve. No! I would not leave!"

"I swear by Time, you will be at the losing end, my friend. If you are still reluctant, I will not force you. We part our ways here."

"Yours is the path. Mine is the place."

The silkworm is disappointed that its friend is reluctant to follow. It leaves without any further word.

The entire inhabitants of the net witness a silkworm climb the twig that points to the roof of the net. At the end of the net is the opening to the vastness of nature that it has always dreamed of.

Reflected in the eyes of every inhabitant of the net is the end that will confront the brave silkworm. It will be treated as those which are sick, squeezed to death by the hands.

But night turns to daytime and promises change hands.

On a bright morning, a moth is seen perching on a piece of silk kimono hanging on the clothes line. It flaps its wings gently and gracefully.

The silk kimono which is a national symbol fades against the light that emanates from the wings of the moth.

12

The Bull

Materialism fed on the soul like leprosy devouring the body. It was not felt but the skin and sinews hardened and died.

He fiddled with the rosary beads, but his soul was devoid of spiritual awakening. He forced himself to meditate but his focus fell like the rosary beads released from their string, the knot broken by his hardened fingers.

He had lost everything. It would be expected that with the loss of all material things, his soul would soar to seek redemption. But the enslaved soul had resulted in a weak and heavy self. He was helpless. Now he realised that what was meant by materialism was not just to own but to be subjugated by yearns that were not part of the soul. He was tormented.

Hot. That was the scene perceived by the players at the stock exchange. The index of his stocks changed vigorously akin to the thousands of dollars that filled his pockets, as energetic as his gaze that was stuck on the billboards in the stock exchange building. His soul was chasing the bull run.

Within ten minutes, he had accrued half a million dollars. But he did not want to let go. His soul was riding the back of the bull that was attacking the stock index with an incredible force.

His stock index was shining with the dollar sign until it exploded victoriously at the final assault of the bull run at the end of trading. He had done it. The heaving sigh of two million dollars almost suffocated him. His body slipped onto the floor like a tired bull. His mouth was frothy with saliva.

He breathed in deeply. Today was hot. But he was still not satisfied. Tomorrow would be hotter. He yearned for the Lexus that would be parked at his home to replace the Hyundai that he had sold to get the money to play with the stocks. He dreamt of the bungalow that would replace the apartment that he had mortgaged to add on to his betting capacity.

He was willing to part temporarily with everything that he owned. He was confident of his ability to read the market trends. He was sure of the strength of the bull that he had reared in his mind. And that night, he snored like a victorious bull.

The next day, after taking a bath, he felt pain at the top right and left of his head. It felt like slight bumps. His eyes were bloodshot, possibly due to insufficient sleep.

Without wasting any time, he rushed to the stock exchange building again. His bull had started running. With a bet of two million dollars, his ambition climbed onto the back of the bull and it was driven to the peak of madness.

His stocks sped like crazy, leaving behind others. He shrieked with joy.

Five million dollars! Five million dollars! He continued chasing the stocks. Seven million dollars! He jumped in ecstasy.

But his joy was muffled by the screams of other players who were gazing at a particular billboard. He rushed towards them. Flashing on the billboard was a stock that was churning thousands of dollars every second.

He tried to read the name of the stock. The frequent flashes of changes to its figure made it difficult to be identified at first. He rubbed his eyes and focused his gaze. The name S.O.U.L. flickered. What is that stock, he wondered. It must be a blue chip. Why had he not noticed it before?

His mind was engulfed by desire. He intended to grab everything, whatever it might take.

Without delay, he called his broker. It was as if his act was driven by a force beyond his control. After listening to his voice, the broker laughed as he could read his intentions. The laughter turned into a shriek that was eerie. The shriek sounded like it had not originated from this earth.

Without hesitation, he put his entire wealth to bet on the stock. He felt like he had also put his breath and life on the bet. His lips quivered as if agreeing on something.

The shriek seeped into his blood vessels until he had goosebumps. Then he felt an excruciating pain on top of his head, like it was pierced and cut by a knife. Now the shriek appeared to originate from his mouth.

He ran towards the washroom. His stomach was queasy. His head felt heavy.

After easing himself, he walked towards the sink. His head was still giddy, his vision blurred. After washing his face, he looked at the mirror. The water droplets on the mirror obscured his sight. He wiped the surface of the mirror with a paper towel.

He rubbed his bloodshot eyes. Suddenly, a bull appeared in front of him. He was shocked and stepped backwards. The hair on his nape stood on ends. He shivered. He gazed at the mirror again. The bull gazed back at him. He looked around. There was nobody in the washroom but him.

He panicked and looked at the mirror again and screamed. Then he shrieked in pain. A pair of horns pierced out through his scalp. Saliva frothed and dripped from his mouth. His hind legs kicked the walls.

Without control, he bashed onto the mirror which broke into pieces and fell on the floor. Suddenly, he heard a series of eerie screams. He felt as if his soul had been pulled out of his body. He was overwhelmed by fear. He crashed into the washroom door and ran towards the main hall of the stock exchange building.

The crowd ran helter-skelter to save their lives when they saw a bull rampaging into the hall. Heaving and panting, he scanned the surroundings. The fearful screams of the crowd reverberated in the hall, confusing his mind. He saw the billboard with its red flickering lights. There was only one stock that was traded.

Portrayed in bright and big capital letters were the alphabets 'S.O.U.L.' The value of that stock was zero, which enlarged and mocked him. He was furious and heaved a heavy breath. His rear legs stamped on the floor.

With rage and revenge, he attacked the billboard. The eerie shriek filled the air again. He became furious and slammed into the billboard with his horns. The billboard broke into pieces. Shards of glass fell onto his shoulders and other parts of his body. His skin and sinews felt as if they were cut into pieces. Warm blood flowed around his neck.

The lights of the smashed board flickered. His well-built body suddenly because rigid. The electric currents from the damaged board flowed into his body and shocked him. Something left his body. He felt weak and fell onto the floor. Darkness engulfed his vision.

Without realisation, materialism had dragged the

soul into destruction and oblivion. It was callous of the soul to be deceived by an unnatural greed, when moderation was its saving grace.

That realisation came too late. His weak breath was already at his throat, his last exhalation.

People said he died in shock. His wide-opened eyes suggested disappointment. His frothing mouth depicted agony. The rosary beads were scattered on the floor.

13

The Sculptor

Who would have expected that he would no longer be able to steer his mind? He had become insane.

Nangonangonang. Ningoningoning.

That was his soul's malady. How was it possible that a gentle and well-adjusted person could have met with such alienation in his life? How was it that the sensitivity that was his gift of personality would rebel against his self? Who would have expected him to become crazy?

Nangonangonang. Ningoningoning.

He was known to be a person who loved life. I remembered an occasion when he scolded me when I gave him a tender piece of wood to be sculpted. I thought that the wood which was still soft and fresh would be easier to be shaped. But to him, my act was that of killing. I had destroyed life as soon as I felled the young mahogany tree.

His love for life emanated from his works – his

figurines breathed life. His eye for detail and refined sculpting reflected his commitment and reverence towards art. The freshness that shone from his sculptures reflected his honesty. He did not like to evade or pretend. He took from life. He gave back to life.

Nangonangonang. Ningoningoning.

I would not be at ease until I understood the reasons for his change. I did not mind the difficulty until I found an answer. I just could not accept the situation.

Thus, I began my search on the basis that there had to be a rational reason for his degradation. That was my faith in reason.

Nangonangonang. Ningoningoning.

I began my search at the factory where he created the figurines. He used to work at a small studio space behind his house. Now he owned a big factory that was equipped with sophisticated machinery and tools, and a large godown for storage.

The main reason for his move from the studio to the factory was because of market demand. His customers had increased considerably.

Where before he was pleased to give away his creations for free, now he was only willing to sell them.

To meet the demands of his customers which had become more pressing, he had to change his system of production. It used to be that he was the only one sculpting. Now he had a team which was divided into different units with specific tasks.

There was a unit that removed the bark from the logs. Another unit sculpted the main body of the figurines, others formed the legs, arms and hands, while another carved the eyes, mouths and ears.

He became the quality controller. He was detached from the process of production. He only accepted or rejected the final products.

Nangonangonang. Ningoningoning.

In short, the sculpting process had been divided up so much that nobody had the opportunity to sculpt an entire figurine. Nobody had the attention and focus for the entire creative process. There was a disconnect in thought and feeling that would give a holistic appreciation of the intent and means.

In fact, my friend had taken from life and had hastened the process of giving back to life. That was my first impression of his enterprise. I was haunted by the desire to see the product that was the result of this modern process.

My desire was diverted by the strong and fragrant aroma that penetrated my nostrils. I recognised the smell to be that of wood sap. I traced the source of the aroma and was brought to a large space. In that open space, I noticed heaps of logs. What struck me was that those logs were from young mahogany trunks.

Now I realised that my friend had not only taken from life, he had snatched it carelessly. I was furious.

But my anger was muddled with a sense of pity. What had happened to my friend?

Nagonangonang. Ningoningoning.

I came to know from the workers that since moving to work at the factory, he was always in a hurry. It was as if he had not a moment to reflect and ponder. That was his favourite pastime before. I could not comprehend fully why this had happened.

Presumably with the efficiency in production, he would have had more time and space for his mind to reflect and ponder. What had caused the diversion of his mind away from life?

I looked around the factory. I was dismayed. Each worker was pre-occupied with their individual tasks. The opportunities to interact had increased but most of the time they interacted only as workers, not as human beings.

Nangonangonang. Ningoningoning.

My friend used to pause from his work and would return home to his wife for lunch and to play with his children. Then he would resume his work. But now, with what I have seen at the factory, I was not so sure he had kept to this routine.

Suddenly, a bell rang. Like awakened figurines, the workers stopped work and left the factory. Their tired faces did not reflect any joy, their eyes were dead. It was as if their souls had hardened. Was the bell the cause?

Nangonangonang. Ningoningoning.

I became restless. The factory stifled my soul but I could not leave just yet. I had to look for the answer to my quandary.

A supervisor passed by me as if I was not there. I stopped him and asked about my friend.

According to him, my friend had become berserk after finding out that the stocks he had placed his money on had plunged. That bad news shook his soul.

Although the supervisor's explanation made sense, I could not fathom nor accept it fully. It was just impossible that my friend, who had loved beauty all his life, could be shaken by something like the plunging of stock market shares.

Who would expect him to become insane from such an incident?

My desire to see the figurines which were the product of the factory production took hold of me. I walked towards the godown with the supervisor.

What I discovered there was beyond expectation and disturbed my peace.

At every nook and corner of the godown stood the figurines. I was aghast to notice that each one of them resembled my friend. In one corner was a computer, which projected a hologram of my friend.

I was dumbstruck and stood still like a figurine. A deep remorse filled my heart.

Nangonangonang. Ningoningoning.

The supervisor informed me that the factory would be shut down because business was bad. I suggested that the factory operations be kept open. But the figurines had to be replaced with human beings.

14

The Merlion

"Dear Mermaid, why are you crying?"

"I cannot take it anymore, Lion."

"Do you hate me, Mermaid?"

"I don't blame you."

"Actually, Mermaid, I cannot take it, too. But what can we do? We are forced to be united. Is this fate?"

"Why are you quick to surrender to fate, Lion?"

"Isn't that what it is?"

"No! What ought to be is that your abode is in the jungle and mine is in the ocean. Not by the fringe of this brutal city!"

The sea breeze caresses the hair of a maiden who is waiting for her love. Her eyes gaze at the lonesome Merlion.

"It's true, Mermaid. I long for life in the jungle. There, I was free to roam. Do you know, Mermaid, I was the king of the jungle and every animal adored and was afraid of me. But here, I was made to be a decoration with you. While I might still look courageous, I cannot prove it. It was heartless of the hunter to have trapped me here!"

"Please don't repeat the incident. I am still hurt."

"You must learn to use your rational faculty like me. Only then would your emotions be stable."

"Don't you understand, I am Mermaid, the queen of emotions who swims in the ocean of life. It's only natural that I act based on my emotions, just as it's your calling to act based on your thoughts."

"Perhaps that is true. Perhaps it was because of this that we were captured and trapped by humans here."

"But humans don't understand our way of life. I am Mermaid, who struggles with the waves. I am Mermaid, who is capable of diving to the depths of the ocean of life to discover the gentleness and secrets of goodness. And you, you are Lion, who governs the mind and its wilderness. You are the guardian of instincts and actions. It was heartless of human beings to unite me with you at this desolate fringe of life. I am suffering from this unholy union."

The maiden smiles widely with the arrival of the young man. The young man holds the maiden's hand. The maiden hugs the young man.

"Have you been waiting long?"

"For you, I'd wait till the end of time."

The waves smash its regrets on the hard rocks. Leaves fall in the wind.

"Dear Mermaid, we don't have a choice. Let's make the best of the situation and learn to live like this. Although our union is unholy because it's not based on willingness and rights, we must accept it with perseverance."

"I expect your mind would find the resolution and truth, but you have not bothered to think thoroughly and deeply. Look at how your current way of life has influenced your behaviour. You have given up your rights. You are no longer courageous like before."

The couple gaze at the sculpture of the Merlion by the park. On such a chilly and dark night, it is easier to be immodest.

"How deep is your love for me?"

"Look at the Merlion. Let it be a symbol of our love. The Lion and the Mermaid as a symbol of you and me. A symbol of our eternal love."

"Are you truthful in what you say?"

"Do you doubt me?"

"How far would you go to prove it to me?"

"As far as you would allow me."

The raging waves become restless. The shore has let itself be conquered.

"You are too engrossed with your emotions, Mermaid. You surely know a stable life cannot be based on mere emotions."

"Are you denying my existence? Or are you ridiculing my purpose in life? Don't you realise, Lion, it's emotions that refine thoughts. Without emotions, thoughts would become savage."

"So now, do you fully accept the truth that we must co-exist?"

"Existence is not life, Lion. In any case, our forced union is unholy. The Creator has given guidance on our marriage. Not based on coercion. Not based on mere desire. But based on truth and sacred love. Your mind and my heart must adhere to His guidance. With this complete surrender, we will find our true freedom."

A small boat glides on the surface of the dark water. The sanctity of the night is adulterated by the presence of the boat that journeys to and from the mouth and end of the river.

"I've proven my love to you. I hope you will be responsible for it."

"Do you still doubt me? Let the Merlion be our witness that you are my one and only love."

The raging waves have subsided. The Merlion becomes muted. The night breeze whispers its sad song in the crevices of the rocks.

The city will hear the cry of an illegitimate child called humanity.

15

Rendezvous

The city is small not because of its size. The city is compact because of the bustling of people connected by computers and satellites, and corporations riding on information technology.

But, regardless of how sophisticated life in this city has become, the city dwellers cannot escape from the basic need to eat. Yes, to eat! A task that begins from feeding and ends in swallowing. And eating is capable of rendezvous. At least, the rendezvous between food and throat.

A habit that has resulted from automation and perhaps laziness is the pastime of city dwellers to visit restaurants. At the restaurants, food has been prepared. All that is needed is to shove it with a fork or spoon into the mouth. Emmm! Simple, but not necessarily tasty and satisfying.

"Where are we going?"

"To answer our desire to survive."

"Is it where artists like you always meet?"

"It's where humanity gathers. And I attest to it."

Amongst the many restaurants in the city, there is one that is most famous. It's often crowded.

"Do they come here often?"

"Whenever they feel empty."

As a reporter for a culinary magazine, I am assigned to investigate the secrets of the restaurant's success. Is it because of the automation of food processing and preparation? Is it due to its 21st century atmosphere or its futuristic menu? I am intrigued, but maybe it is due to my empty stomach. I must accomplish this task before I eat.

"Why do you always come here?"

"Here, my paint brush discovers colour and movement."

"Is it compelling for you?"

"It's like breathing to me, more than a habit."

And since I have been assigned to do a scoop on the restaurant, I am belaboured by a habit which I cannot control. My eyelids flutter involuntarily, and I hear strange sounds that make my ears damp. The sound is so primal.

Tis. Tis. Tis.

"Do you like to paint here?"

"The paint drips from my brush are like the drizzle that comes uninvited."

That sound is like the rain droplets that fall from the

tips of an attap thatch roof that is now just a memory. It is a memory that is best forgotten because time has changed in this modern city.

"In this sophisticated age, people do not appreciate art like your painting."

"It's not art that they reject. What is discarded is life."

So, I contact the restaurant with the app in my handphone. The screen remains blue and silent. I cannot reach the restaurant through the Internet. I try again, but still no response. Damn! This is not what I have planned. And I do not like my plans to be disrupted. Life must be planned. Automation eases plans. The restaurant is creating difficulties for my task, and it chides at my ability to think and judge.

"Doesn't thinking complete life?"

"What is fulfilled are plans and rules, not room for life."

"Do you reject them?"

"I prefer the wind and rain."

I rush in a taxi which I book through my phone app. I direct the taxi driver to take the shortest route in the quickest time. With IT and automation, that is easy. In less than five minutes, I have reached my destination. But I am dumbfounded by what I see.

"But plans and rules create convenience."

"Plans and rules suffocate. People are entrapped in time and space that are planned and pursued."

And I still cannot believe it. Is this really the famous restaurant? It is crowded, and people are lining up outside the building. But it does not portray the sophistication and fame that are touted. It looks dilapidated and messy. Its design is old-school. The advertisement boards are archaic, only paint on a wooden board. The mystery that surrounds the restaurant makes me uneasy and curious.

"Do you like life that is not ordered?"

"I like things that are natural, like fallen leaves and dew that drips from branches."

Tis. Tis. Tis.

My eyelids begin to flutter again. The image of its customers is even stranger, which is unbefitting of the restaurant's. They look like technocrats, bureaucrats and members of corporations of the super-computer age. They are inheritors of a culture nurtured by sophisticated thinking that has buried whatever remains of feelings that would thwart their plans and actions.

"Look around. There's none like you."

"There is, although he has not realised it himself."

"Who?"

"He records life. He will step into this place."

They are all in suits and ties, and carry laptops. Many are busy looking at their electronic planners to ensure all meetings and tasks are carried out successfully according to schedule, including the time to eat, at this dilapidated restaurant, nonetheless.

"What's the same between you and him?"

"We are both hungry and searching."

Now my stomach is grumbling. I remember I have not eaten.

Tis. Tis. Tis.

That sound comes from my stomach, perhaps from the acid that drips from it because it is not filled with food yet. I rush into the restaurant.

"Do you like to spend time here?"

"Just to fill in time, to relish tranquillity amidst chaos."

As soon as I step into the restaurant, I am befuddled. It is chaotic. Customers push and are pushed without care and concern. They step onto and chide each other. I feel like I am one of the ingredients of the food that is prepared. It is stuffy and hot. I cannot breathe.

I feel I am being stir-fried in a pot. A cultural pot that is so strange. But the incessant fluttering of my eyelids reminds me that I have visited this place before.

"Do you mean that reporter?"

"You are observant. Here, our three hearts meet."

Suddenly, I feel the urge to crawl. My head is spinning, and I have to move slowly. The restaurant is filled with smoke.

I track the source of the smoke. I see a furnace that is fed with wood and charcoal. I smell something primal, like the smell of a newborn baby or death that drips from the smouldering smoke. It is certain that, whatever is in the pot, is not fully cooked yet.

Tis. Tis. Tis.

"Why do you let the paint drip freely?"

"The paint drips are seeking space to meet on the canvas of life."

The sauce flows over the pot in the furnace. My eyelids flutter continuously. What kind of food is boiled in the pot?

The technocrats are greedily devouring the food. The bureaucrats are fighting to be served first. Members of corporations lose their way at one corner of the restaurant. It is as if all plans and rules are abandoned as they behave like children.

"I can't believe that such sophisticated people would behave as such."

"Let them be. They are interesting subjects for my paintings. They have actually forgotten that they were once droplets, like the paint from my brush."

Tis. Tis. Tis.

The saliva from their mouths drip onto the table and floor. They are devouring the food that is seemingly delicious. And there is something else besides saliva that is dripping incessantly.

Tis. Tis. Tis. Tis. Tis.

They are crying. I am, too. I am shocked when I see that my heart is served on the plate. It is floundering about with the historical and cultural ingredients of my life.

I turn my head. There is an artist with his friend. My bleeding heart has become the subject of his painting.

He just smiles and sprinkles red paint onto the canvas. The red paint then drips onto the floor.

Tis. Tis. Tis.

"Why are there tears in your eyes?"

"I'm delighted at this rendezvous, especially when it is incidental."

I gaze at the blood that flows from my heart. It has been suffering from the stabs of automation, bureaucracy and corporate culture. I have never thought of relishing my own heart. It is obvious that there are more basic things than planning, rules and eating habits.

I realise that they come here to mourn their wounded hearts. I do, too. And I still remember when I was born, I cried first before I was fed with milk.

Tis. Tis. Tis.

I lose my appetite. I request the waiter to pack the food for me to bring back home. I step out of the restaurant, gingerly carrying my humanity that is uncooked.

"Shall we follow the reporter?"

"We follow his steps, but it's not necessary to greet him. We have met."

Appendix

Sources of first publication:

1 The Orchid
"Anggerik" in *Singathology* (NAC and Marshall Cavendish International (Asia), 2015) Vol 1 – new English translation

2 The Bargaining
"Permintaan" in *Catatan Perjalanan* (Marshall Cavendish, 2017) – new English translation

3 Glass
"Kaca" in *Celupan* (KL: Al-Ameen Serve Holdings, 2010)

4 Green Man Plus
"Green Man Plus" in *Fish Eats Lion* (Epigram, 2012) – original story written in English

5 Otai
"Otai" in *Singathology* (NAC and Marshall Cavendish International (Asia), 2015) Vol 2 – new English translation

6 The Gardener
"Pekebun" in *Celupan* (KL: Al-Ameen Serve Holdings, 2010)

7 The Clinic
"Klinik" in *Celupan* (KL: Al-Ameen Serve Holdings, 2010)

8 Door
"Pintu" in *Celupan* (KL: Al-Ameen Serve Holdings, 2010)

9 The Architect
"Arkitek" in *Celupan* (KL: Al-Ameen Serve Holdings, 2010)

10 The Mimbar
New story written in English

11 The Crucible
"Celupan" in *Celupan* (KL: Al-Ameen Serve Holdings, 2010)

12 The Bull
"Seladang" in *Celupan* (KL: Al-Ameen Serve Holdings, 2010)

13 The Sculptor
"Pengukir" in *Celupan* (KL: Al-Ameen Serve Holdings, 2010)

14 The Merlion
"Arca" in *Celupan* (KL: Al-Ameen Serve Holdings, 2010)

15 Rendezvous
"Pertemuan" in *Celupan* (KL: Al-Ameen Serve Holdings, 2010)

About the Author

Isa Kamari has written 11 novels, three collections of poetry, a collection of short stories, a book of essays on Singapore Malay poetry, a collection of theatre scripts and lyrics of three song albums. His novels in Malay have been translated into English, Turkish, Urdu, Arabic, Indonesian, Jawi, Russian, Spanish, French and Mandarin. His collections of essays and selected poems have been translated into English. His first novel in English, *Tweet*, was published in 2016. Isa was conferred the Southeast Asia Write Award from Thailand in 2006, the Singapore Cultural Medallion in 2007, the Anugerah Tun Seri Lanang from the Singapore Malay Language Council in 2009 and the Mastera Literary Award from Brunei Darussalam in 2018.